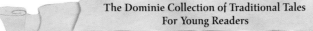
The Dominie Collection of Traditional Tales
For Young Readers

The Musicians of Bremen

Retold by Alan Trussell-Cullen

Illustrated by Eric Rowe

Dominie Press, Inc.

Once upon a time, there was a donkey. He had lived and worked on a farm for many years. But now he was old and weak, and the farmer wanted to get rid of him.

It so happened that the donkey loved music. He loved to sing, and he was sure he had a beautiful voice.

"*Ee-aw! Ee-aw!*" he sang all day.

The donkey had heard that there were many wonderful bands making music in the town of Bremen. He decided to run away to Bremen and join a band.

On the way to Bremen, he met an old dog.

"What's the matter with you?" asked the donkey.

"My master says I am too old to help on the farm," said the dog. "He wants to get rid of me."

"Why don't you come with me?" said the donkey. "I'm going to Bremen to sing in a band."

"*Woof! Woof!*" sang the dog. "I have a good voice, too. I'll come to Bremen and join a band with you."

A little farther down the road, they met an old cat.

"What's the matter with you?" asked the donkey.

"My master says I am too old to catch mice," said the cat. "He wants to get rid of me."

"Why don't you come with us?" said the donkey. "We're going to Bremen to sing in a band."

"*Mee-ow!*" sang the cat. "I have a good voice, too. I'll come to Bremen and join a band with you."

A little farther down the road, they came upon an old rooster.

"What's the matter with you?" asked the donkey.

"My master says I am too old for the farm," said the rooster. "He wants to get rid of me."

"Why don't you come with us?" said the donkey. "We're going to Bremen to sing in a band."

"*Cock-a-doodle-doo!*" sang the rooster. "I have a good voice, too. I'll come to Bremen and join a band with you."

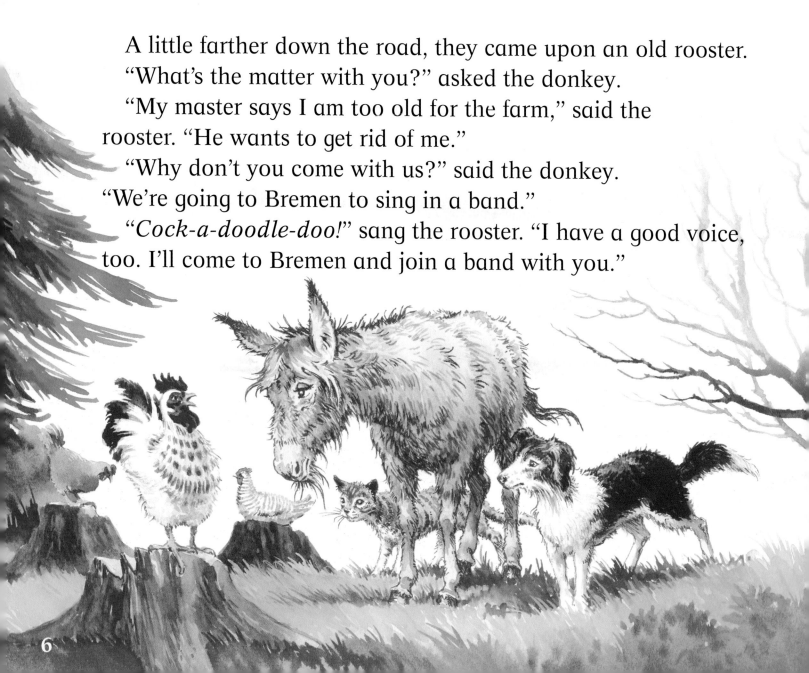

Soon they found themselves in a forest. It was beginning to grow dark. They saw a house through the trees. There were lights in the windows.

"Perhaps we could go and sing to the people in that house," said the donkey.

"They might be so pleased with our sweet voices that they would invite us in to stay the night."

Now, inside the house were three robbers. They were busy counting all their loot.

They had piles of gold and silver coins, as well as a fine meal.

The four musicians stood outside the window.
They cleared their throats and began to sing.
   "Ee-aw! Ee-aw!"
   "Woof! Woof! Woof! Woof!"
   "Mee-ow! Mee-ow!"
   "Cock-a-doodle-doo!"

9

The robbers got a terrible fright!
They thought there was a dreadful monster making all the noise.
They dropped all their loot and ran for their lives.

10

The four friends made their way inside the house.
They were very surprised to find the house empty.
They were very hungry, so they sat down and
began to eat.

After the meal they were tired, so they decided to go to sleep for the night.

The donkey found some straw in the yard.

The dog lay down on the mat behind the door.

The cat curled up by the fireplace.

The rooster perched on the rafters.

Later in the night, the robbers crept back to the house.
They saw there were no lights on.
One of the robbers decided to creep inside to see if the monster had gone.
He tiptoed into the kitchen.

He couldn't see a thing, so he decided to light a match on the hot coals he could see glowing in the fireplace. But they weren't hot coals at all! They were the eyes of the cat glowing in the dark. When the robber held the match stick to her eyes, the cat spat at him and scratched his arm.

"Help!" roared the robber as he stumbled backward and stepped on the dog.

The dog leaped up and bit him on the leg.

"Help! Help!" shouted the robber as he ran out into the yard.

There he ran straight into the donkey, who kicked him with his hooves.
"Help! Help! Help!" shouted the robber.

Meanwhile, all this noise had woken the rooster, who began to crow from the rafters!

"*Cock-a-doodle-doo! Cock-a-doodle-doo!*"

"Help! Help! Help! Help!" shouted the robber as he ran back to join the others.

"We can't go back in there!" he said. "There's a witch in the house. She spat at me and scratched me with her long, bony fingernails!
And then a man with a knife tried to stab me in the leg!
And then a monster in the yard hit me with a club!
And then a goblin sitting on top of the house started shouting, 'Cook him in a stew! Cook him in a stew!' "

So the robbers never went back to the house. And the
four friends were so happy, they decided to live there
and make music together for the rest of their lives.

Publisher: Raymond Yuen
Editor: John S. F. Graham
Designer: Greg DiGenti
Illustrator: Eric Rowe

Published by:

℗ **Dominie Press, Inc.**

1949 Kellogg Avenue
Carlsbad, California 92008 USA

Paperback ISBN 0-7685-0332-9
Library Bound Edition ISBN 0-7685-1694-3
Printed in Singapore by PH Productions Pte Ltd

10 11 12 V0ZF 14 13 12 11 10